What could & be better than this?

LINDA ASHMAN

paintings by LINDA S. WINGERTER

DUTTON CHILDREN'S BOOKS

DUTTON CHILDREN'S BOOKS
A DIVISION OF PENGUIN YOUNG READERS GROUP

PUBLISHED BY THE PENGUIN GROUP / Penguin Group (USA) Inc., 375 Hudson Street, New York, New York 10014, U.S.A. / Penguin Group (Canada), 90 Eglinton Avenue East, Suite 700, Toronto, Ontario, Canada M4P 2Y3 (a division of Pearson Penguin Canada Inc.) / Penguin Books Ltd, 80 Strand, London WC2R 0RL, England / Penguin Ireland, 25 St Stephen's Green, Dublin 2, Ireland (a division of Penguin Books Ltd) / Penguin Group (Australia), 250 Camberwell Road, Camberwell, Victoria 3124, Australia (a division of Pearson Australia Group Pty Ltd) / Penguin Books India Pvt Ltd, 11 Community Centre, Panchsheel Park, New Delhi - 110 017, India / Penguin Group (NZ), Cnr Airborne and Rosedale Roads, Albany, Auckland 1310, New Zealand (a division of Pearson New Zealand Ltd) / Penguin Books (South Africa) (Pty) Ltd, 24 Sturdee Avenue, Rosebank, Johannesburg 2196, South Africa / Penguin Books Ltd, Registered Offices: 80 Strand, London WC2R 0RL, England

LIBRARY OF CONGRESS CATALOGING-IN-PUBLICATION DATA
Ashman, Linda.
What could be better than this? / by Linda Ashman; illustrated by Linda S. Wingerter.
p. cm.
Summary: Although a king and queen lead rich and adventurous lives,
they feel an emptiness until the day their child is born.
ISBN 0-525-46954-0
[1. Parent and child—Fiction. 2. Kings, queens, rulers, etc.—Fiction.
3. Stories in rhyme.] I. Wingerter, Linda S., ill. II. Title.
PZ8.3.A775Wh 2006 [E]—dc21 2003049075

Published in the United States by Dutton Children's Books,
a division of Penguin Young Readers Group, 345 Hudson Street, New York, New York 10014
www.penguin.com/youngreaders

Designed by Heather Wood
Manufactured in China
First Edition 10 9 8 7 6 5 4 3 2 1

To
Jack and Jackson,
with much love

For
Keely and Brian Knudsen,
who lent me their vision
~ l s w

Long, long ago, when your papa was king,
With a fabulous castle and throne,
He spent every day chasing dragons away
And ruled the whole world on his own.

His clothing was splendid.
His carriage was gold.
His gardens and stables a sight to behold.
And yet, despite all the fine things that he had,
He sometimes felt lonely and sad.

Even a king can feel sad.

Back in the days when your mama sailed ships,
Gliding through rough-rolling waves,
She raced after pirates, scared away sharks,
And found buried treasure in caves.

She talked to the pelicans,
Played with the whales,
Climbed to the top of her hundred-foot sails.
But some days she'd gaze at the faraway shore,
Sighing, "Isn't there anything more?"

Her heart yearned for just a bit more.

Once, while the king was inspecting his fleet,
The Great Royal Ship hit a rock.
Now it just so happens your mama was near
And towed the crew back to the dock.

Your papa's eyes sparkled,
Your mama's heart danced.
Clearly, the two were completely entranced.

So, right on the spot, near the opal lagoon,
They married that same afternoon,
Then left on a grand honeymoon.

By day at the castle, they ruled and decreed,
Then danced through the bright, starry nights.

And once in a while they'd pack up their bags
And race off to see the great sights:
The end of the rainbow, the unicorn's home,
The land of the giants, the realm of the gnome.

"Our lives are exciting!" the twosome agreed.
"But still there is something we need.

What more could we possibly need?"

After some years, your papa confessed,
"I'm weary of wearing this crown.
This castle's too busy, the dragons too loud.
I long for a quieter town."

Your mama said, "Yes, I completely agree.
Let's give up our gold and this old castle key.
It's fine being queen, but there's something I miss—
Something much sweeter than this.

We'll find something sweeter than this."

Far from the castle, not so long ago,
You slipped between darkness and light.

Your mama and papa were waiting right there
To hold you and wrap you up tight.
They played with your fingers.
They counted your toes.
They kissed your fine hair and your tiny, round nose.

And leaning in close to your small, perfect ear,
They whispered, "You're finally here.

Our beautiful baby is here."

The first years passed quickly, with so much to learn.
You showed them new wonders each hour:
A smooth-polished pebble, a fiery leaf,
A seashell, a sparrow, a flower.

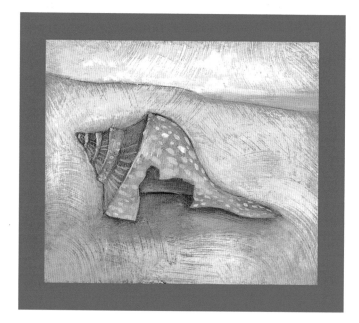

You taught them new languages, new songs to sing,
How to make treasures with feathers and string.

And when they could listen, and move at your pace,
The world had a new sort of grace:

It seemed quite a magical place.

Now when your mama and papa take trips,
You serve as their captain and guide.
You lead them to sea coves where mermaids have been
And forests where leprechauns hide.

They've made a new castle of putty and stone,
Found some new dragons, and built a new throne.

And when the moon shines in your room every night,
They dance with you slowly, then tuck you in tight,

Ending each day with a warm, tender kiss,
Saying, "What could be better than this?"

"Nothing is better than this."